ALL JOIN IN

QUENTIN BLAKE

Mini Treasures

RED FOX

1 3 5 7 9 10 8 6 4 2

Copyright © Quentin Blake 1990

Quentin Blake has asserted his right under the Copyright, Designs and Patents Act, 1988
to be identified as the author and illustrator of this work.

First published in the United Kingdom 1990 by Jonathan Cape Ltd

First published in Mini Treasures edition 1998
by Red Fox
Random House, 20 Vauxhall Bridge Road, London, SW1V 2SA

Random House Australia (Pty) Ltd
20 Alfred Street, Milsons Point, Sydney, New South Wales 2061, Australia

Random House New Zealand Limited
18 Poland Road, Glenfield, Auckland 10, New Zealand

Random House South Africa
PO Box 2263, Rosebank 2121, South Africa

RANDOM HOUSE UK Limited Reg No. 954009

ISBN 0 099 263 53 X

Printed in Singapore

In This Book

Important Message
YOU CAN JOIN IN
TOO

for Linda

All Join In

When Sandra plays the trumpet
it makes a lovely sound

And Mervyn on his drum-kit
can be heard for
miles around

Stephanie is brilliant
when she plays the violin

But the very best of all is when
we ALL JOIN IN

When Amy throws a tantrum
it is wonderful to see

And when Eric starts his wailing
there is noise enough for three

When Bernard kicks the dustbin
it really makes a din

But the very best of all is when
we ALL JOIN IN

The Hooter Song

When William's in his study
    and his thoughts are very deep
We come and help him concentrate –

We go BEEP-BEEP BEEP-BEEP

When Lilian sings a sad song
  and we think she's going to weep
We like to come and cheer her up –

We go BEEP-BEEP BEEP-BEEP

When Oscar's on the sofa
    and he's curled up fast asleep
We know he likes a serenade –

We go BEEP-BEEP BEEP-BEEP

Nice Weather for Ducks

We're all off to the river
    along the muddy track
And we're joining in the
    Duck Song
    QUACK QUACK QUACK

We each have our umbrella
    and our wellies and our mack
And we're joining in the Duck Song
    QUACK QUACK QUACK

We don't care if it's raining
and the sky is murky black –
We're joining in the duck song
QUACKQUACKQUACKQUACKQUACK

Sliding

It's cold and wet and dark outside
In here we'll have a lovely slide
All down the banisters –

WHEEEE!

It's large and grey and lots of fun
We're sliding down it one by one
All down the elephant –

WHEEEEEE!

We're in the wind and sun and snow
Let's see how fast our sledge will go
All down the mountainside –

WHEEEEEEEE!

BUMP!

Sorting Out the Kitchen Pans

We're sorting out the Kitchen Pans
  DING DONG BANG
Sorting out the Kitchen Pans
  BING BONG CLANG

Sorting out the Kitchen Pans
TING BANG DONG
Sorting out the Kitchen Pans
CLANG DING BONG

Sorting out the Kitchen Pans
DONG DANG BONG
TING TANG BING BANG
CLANG DING

OW

Bedtime Song

The stars above are glittering
The moon is gleaming bright
And noisy cats are singing songs
Down in the yard tonight
MIAOW WOW WOW
WOW WOW

People in their dressing-gowns
In houses far and near
Are leaning from their window sills
They're horrified to hear
MIAOW WOW WOW
WOW WOW

But we don't want a lullaby
    We prefer a din
Noisy cats are what we like –
All join in!
        MIAOW WOW WOW
                WOW WOW
                    WOW WOW

All Join In

When we're cleaning up the house
We ALL JOIN IN

When we're trying to catch a mouse
We ALL JOIN IN

When we've got some tins of paint
We **ALL JOIN IN**

And when Granny's going to faint
We ALL JOIN IN

And if Ferdinand decides to make
a chocolate fudge banana cake
What do we do? For goodness sake!

We
ALL JOIN IN